DATE DUE

APR 17	DEC 1 1 1997	FEB 0 8 2005	
		FEB 1 7 2005	
		MAR 1 6 2005	
FEB 2 5 1998		MAY 1 3 2005	
11/3		SEP 0 6 2005	
11/16 Katie		NOV 1 5 2005	
12/16		AUG 3 1 2006	
2/25		FEB 1 6 2007	
4/28		APR 1 4 2007	
3-27-01		NOV 0 2 2007	
NOV 2 1 2002		FEB 1 1 2008	
JAN 1 5 2004			
FEB 1 7 2004			
SEP 0 2 2004			
SEP 0 8 2004			
OCT 2 7 2004			
JAN 2 8 2005			

DEMCO 38-296

M

Hello!
We're the Care Bears

We're a special group of colorful, round, snuggly little bears whose job it is to help you understand your own feelings and share them with others.

As you can see, we have special pictures on our tummies, and those pictures tell you the special job each of us loves to do.

I'm Tenderheart Bear, and it's my job to help people reach out to each other. I say that love is a warm, fuzzy feeling, so go ahead and share it.

I'm Cheer Bear, and if you're sad or not feeling well, I'll slide down a rainbow and make you feel better.

Smile! I'm Funshine Bear, so there's a great, big, happy sun on my tummy to remind you to laugh and look at the lighter side of things.

You're in luck 'cause it's me, Good Luck Bear. That's why I'm wearing a four-leaf clover.

Don't count the number of birthdays.
Count how happy you feel. I'm Birthday
Bear, and I'll help make your birthdays
the best ever.

I'm Wish Bear, and if
you wish on my star,
maybe your special dream
will come true.

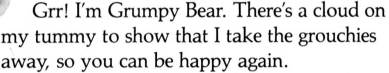

If you're ever feeling lonely,
just call on me, Friend Bear.
See, I've got a daisy for you
and a daisy for me.

Grr! I'm Grumpy Bear. There's a cloud on
my tummy to show that I take the grouchies
away, so you can be happy again.

I'm Love-a-Lot Bear. I have two
hearts on my tummy. One is for you;
the other is for someone you love.

It's my job to bring you sweet dreams.
I'm Bedtime Bear, and right now I'm a bit
sleepy. Are you sleepy, too?

Now that you know all of us, we hope
that you'll have a special place for us in your
heart, just like we do for you.

With love from all of us,

The Care Bears

CHILDRENS PRESS CHOICE

A Parker Brothers title selected for educational distribution

ISBN 0-516-09012-7

Library of Congress Cataloging in Publication Data: Main entry under title: The Care Bears' book of favorite bedtime stories.
SUMMARY: A collection of folklore, fairy tales, fables, and poems selected from the most famous in children's literature.
1. Children's literature.   2. Tales.   [1. Literature—Collections.   2. Folklore.]
PZ5.C1826   1984   808.8'99282   [E]   83-23656   ISBN 0-910313-20-2
Manufactured in the United States of America   4 5 6 7 8 9 0

Care Bears

Book of Favorite Bedtime Stories

Pictures by
Tom Cooke   Troy Howell
Leslie H. Morrill   Stella Ormai
Bob Pepper   David Wiesner

ello there! My name is Bedtime Bear, and if there is one thing that I like better than anything else, it's a good bedtime story. That's why I thought of this book — because I and the other Care Bears know that reading or listening to one of your favorite stories or poems can make bedtime an extra-special, snuggly time.

In the first story the farmer's son has a cat as his best friend, and no one could ask for a better one. I like this story because of Puss in boots' clever trick at the end. Are you ready to hear about it? Then settle down, get tucked in tight and turn the page.

Puss in Boots

ONCE UPON A TIME a poor farmer died and left nothing to his son except a wretched little farm that could hardly grow a thing and a fine black cat.

"Alas," moaned the farmer's son. "What am I to do with such an inheritance? I might as well lie down and let a coach run over me, for surely I have no bright future."

The cat, who heard the young man talking, looked at him shrewdly and said, "Master, I know how to help you. If you give me a sack and a pair of boots such as a fine gentleman wears, you will find that you are better off than you suppose."

The farmer's son did not really believe what the cat had said, but he was so surprised to hear a cat speak that he did as the animal requested. He found a sack and bought a small pair of fine boots and gave them to the cat. The cat put on the boots, slung the sack across his shoulders, and marched out of the farmhouse.

The cat went only a little way before he came to a rabbit hole. He put some lettuce leaves in his bag and then stretched himself out beside it, remaining so still that anyone would have thought that he was dead. Soon the rabbits became curious and hopped up to the bag. One of them saw the lettuce leaves and went into the bag to nibble them. Quick as a flash the cat jumped up and caught the plump rabbit in the bag. Then the cat marched straight to the castle and asked to speak to the king. The king was allowing people to approach him that day, so the cat was permitted into the throne room.

Puss in boots bowed low and said, "Sire, my master, the Lord of Montvale, has asked me to bring you this plump hare, for he knows that you love a good rabbit stew."

"Tell your master that I am very pleased with this gift," replied the king.

Two days later the cat played the trick again on two fat pheasants, and the king was so pleased with the gift that he ordered that the cat be taken to the kitchen and given a bowl of the tastiest cream in the kingdom.

A week later Puss in boots heard that the king was going to take a drive by the river. Puss ran to his master and said, "Hurry; go bathe in the river at the spot I show you, and leave all the rest to me. Just remember that if anyone asks who you are, tell them you are the Lord of Montvale."

The farmer's son, who was still as poor as ever, was surprised at this instruction. But he decided to obey the cat, and he jumped into the river.

While the farmer's son was swimming the king passed nearby. He was startled to hear a cry, "Help! Help! the Lord of Montvale is drowning!" The king put his head out of his carriage and saw Puss in boots, who told him that his master had been robbed of all his clothes and thrown into the river. The king was shocked to hear the news. He had his footmen rescue the surprised young man and immediately ordered a fine set of clothes sent from the palace. The farmer's son put them on and came to thank the king for his kindness. He was very handsome. The king and his daughter the princess, who was traveling with him, were much impressed. They offered him a ride in their carriage, and he accepted.

Puss in boots was very pleased by this turn of events. He ran ahead of the carriage until he came to a bunch of workers mowing a field. "Hello, good people," said the cat in a very serious voice. "The king will soon be coming along. You are to wave to him, and when he stops, tell him that this field and those as far as the eye can see belong to the Lord of Montvale. If you do not, you will be chopped up into millions of tiny pieces."

The workers did as they were told, and the king was much impressed. Puss in boots continued along, telling everyone that he met the same sort of thing, until the king was convinced that the Lord of Montvale must be one of the most wealthy and powerful men who lived in his kingdom.

Finally, Puss in boots came to a grand palace where he knew a fierce ogre lived. The cat knocked at the door, and when the ogre came to answer it the cat said, "I come from my Lord of Montvale. He says that you must meet him for a duel because you are such a weak thing that he cannot stand the thought of you."

"Weak, am I?" roared the ogre. "Does he not know that I can change shapes at will and become anything I want to be?" And with that he changed into an enormous, fire-breathing dragon.

Puss in boots watched and waited and then said in a very bored tone, "Ah, well, that is all very good, but there are many ogres who can turn themselves into something huge. I wonder if you can turn yourself into something small."

"Just wait and see," hissed the ogre. In the wink of an eye he changed himself into a very small mouse.

Puss in boots licked his whiskers and jumped at once on the mouse and ate it up. As the king's carriage passed by the gates of the palace, the clever cat was there, bowing and motioning for the party to come in. When the king and his company entered, Puss in boots told them that the Lord of Montvale owned the palace and that they were welcome. Now the farmer's son was amazed to hear this, but he trusted his cat and so said nothing.

The king entered and was given such a fine meal that he became even more impressed with the man he thought to be the Lord of Montvale. Before the evening was over he had offered the hand of his daughter in marriage. This pleased both the farmer's son and the princess, and soon they were married. They lived happily ever after. As for Puss in boots, he lived a life of luxury, chasing mice and drinking as much rich cream as he desired.

ou know me, I'm Birthday Bear. I always like to have a snack whenever I can, but it seems to me that the wolf in this story wanted the wrong kind of snack. I'm afraid he learns the hard way not to try to eat the things he shouldn't. I wish someone had told me that before I ate three helpings of ice cream!

Little Red Riding Hood

ONCE UPON A TIME there was a little girl who always wore a red cloak, so she was called Little Red Riding Hood by everyone who knew her. One day Little Red Riding Hood's mother called to her and said, "Your beloved grandmother, who lives on the other side of the woods, is not feeling very well. Here, take this basket of goodies to her. Do not play along the way, and above all do not get into conversations with strangers as you go through the woods."

Little Red Riding Hood agreed, and she skipped off into the woods, glad to be of some use to her mother.

When she got into the woods, Little Red Riding Hood met a wolf, and, forgetting entirely what her mother had said, she stopped to talk to him. She did not know what a wicked animal he was, so she felt no fear.

"Good morning, Little Red Riding Hood," said the wolf. "Where are you going so early?"

"Good morning, wolf," she said. "I am off to my grandmother's with this basket of goodies that I hope she will enjoy."

"And where, pray tell, does your grandmother live?" the wolf asked.

"About two miles farther down this path, right near a grove of large oak trees," Red Riding Hood answered.

The wolf thought to himself, "Now I could eat this child up right here and also feast on her basket of goodies. However, if I go to the grandmother's house, I can make a meal of them both!" He excused himself and ran quickly down the path to Red Riding Hood's grandmother's house. He knocked on the door, and when the old woman asked who it was, the wolf replied, "Little Red Riding Hood, come to bring you a basket of goodies." The old woman opened the door, and the wolf rushed in, meaning to eat her up. The grandmother was a spry old woman, however, and she ran away from the wolf and hid herself behind a locked cellar door.

The wolf was worried that Little Red Riding Hood would soon be approaching, so he quickly dressed himself in one of the grandmother's nightgowns and climbed into her bed. Sure enough, before long Little Red Riding Hood was at the door.

"Come in," said the wolf in what he hoped was a voice like an old grandmother.

Red Riding Hood opened the door and approached the bed. She felt frightened, but she did not quite know why. She went up to the wolf and looked at him.

"Oh, grandmother, what big ears you have," she said.

"The better to hear you, my dear," the wolf answered.

"Oh, grandmother, what big eyes you have."

"The better to see you, my dear."

"Oh, grandmother, what big *teeth* you have."

"The better to *eat* you with, my dear!"

And saying this, the wolf sprang out of bed and tried to bite Little Red Riding Hood.

Just at that moment a strong woodsman was passing by. He heard the girl's cries, and ran into the house. Seeing the wolf, he took out his ax and chopped the nasty brute's tail right off.

"Aiee!" yelled the wolf, and he ran out of the house and was never seen again.

As soon as she heard the wolf leave, the grandmother came up from the cellar, and she, the woodsman, and Little Red Riding Hood sat down and ate up all the goodies in the basket.

'm Friend Bear, and here are two stories I think you'll enjoy. The first one is about what happens if you are a friend and help others out. The second, which is told in verse, shows what can happen if you don't try to get along. If the gingham dog and calico cat had used my help, they would have been much better off!

The Bremen Town Musicians

ONCE UPON A TIME an old donkey ran away from his cruel master
and decided to seek his fortune in the town of Bremen. He thought
that he might get a job there as a street musician. He was walking down
the road when he came upon an aged hound lying by the side of the road
whining.

"Well, old fellow, what can be the trouble?" asked the donkey.

"As I became older, I found that I was too tired to hunt," the hound
replied. "So my master was going to have me killed. I ran away, but now
I have no idea how to make my living."

"Why don't you come with me?" asked the donkey. "I am going to
Bremen to become a musician. You could take up music too. I will sing, and
you can play the drum."

The dog agreed, and the pair walked on together. Soon they came upon
a cat who looked miserable.

"Hello there, old whiskers," said the donkey. "Why are you looking
so glum?"

"What is there to be happy about?" the cat answered. "I became stiff
in my joints as I aged, and I wanted to sit by the fire rather than chase mice.
My mistress grew impatient with my behavior and wanted to drown me,
so I ran away. Alas, I do not know what will become of me."

"Come with us to Bremen," said the dog. "I know you have the
makings of a fine musician."

The cat thought that this was a splendid idea, and so she went along with the other travelers.

By and by the three new friends passed a farmyard where a rooster was crowing with all his might.

"You should only be crowing at break of day," said the cat. "Why do you carry on so now that it is afternoon?"

"I am upset," replied the rooster. "I have served my master well these past ten years, but now he is entertaining a very important guest, and I heard him say that I should be put into a soup. Do you blame me for crowing so loudly?"

"You had better come with us to Bremen," said the donkey. "We are going to be musicians, and your powerful voice will be perfect."

The rooster agreed, and they all traveled on together.

Bremen was a distant city, so it could not be reached in a single day's journey. The travelers agreed to spend the night in a field. However, the dog could not seem to find a comfortable spot to lay his weary bones. He circled round and round, and felt most irritated by his lack of sleep.

As he looked to the west, the dog noticed some bright lights that obviously came from a house at the distant edge of the field.

"Let us go over there," the hound said to the others. "Perhaps they will have a soft mat or a bit of hay on which we can be more comfortable."

They all set off toward the light. At last they reached the house, and the donkey, being the tallest, went and looked in the window. Much to his amazement he saw a band of robbers sitting around a table that was heaped with gold and good things to eat.

He told his companions what he saw, and they became determined to chase the robbers away and live in the house themselves. The animals came up with a plan. The donkey stood by the window. The dog stood on his back with the cat on top of him.

The rooster flew to the very top of this pile, and then all the animals began to sing. The donkey brayed, the dog barked, the cat mewed, and the rooster crowed.

When the robbers heard that terrible sound, they thought they were being attacked by a goblin or some other creature, and they fled in horror.

The four animals went into the house and ate up all the good food. Then they put out the lights and went to sleep. The rooster flew up to a beam in the ceiling and settled down, the cat curled up by the fire, the dog slept on a rug behind the door, and the donkey went outside and lay on the grass.

The robbers had not gone far away, and when they saw that the lights in the house were put out, they decided that the monster had gone away. One of them was sent back to the house in hopes of recovering their gold.

When the robber entered, however, he stepped on the cat's tail. The cat flew at the robber, hissing and scratching. The man ran toward the back door, and the dog barked and bit his leg. He rushed out the door only to be given a good kick by the donkey. The rooster, awakened by the commotion, gave a loud "cock-a-doodle-do."

The robber ran back to the leader of the gang. "Oh, let us leave this place," he cried. "The house is inhabited by a witch whose warm breath and sharp nails I felt on my face. The witch has a troll who helps her, and that creature growled and stabbed me in the leg. To make matters worse, a ghost in the backyard beat me with a club as it screamed some magical chant."

When he heard this, the leader of the robbers led them away. The Bremen town musicians were left free to live in their new little house, and they are there to this day.

The Duel

by Eugene Field

THE GINGHAM DOG and the calico cat
  Side by side on the table sat;
'Twas half-past twelve, and (what do you think!)
Nor one nor t'other had slept a wink!
The old Dutch clock and the Chinese plate
Appeared to know as sure as fate
There was going to be a terrible spat.
(I wasn't there; I simply state
What was told to me by the Chinese plate!)

The gingham dog went, "Bow-wow-wow!"
The calico cat replied, "Mee-ow!"
The air was littered, an hour or so,
With bits of gingham and calico,
While the old Dutch clock in the chimney-place
Up with its hands before its face,
For it always dreaded a family row!
(Now mind: I'm only telling you
What the old Dutch clock declares is true!)

The Chinese plate looked very blue,
And wailed, "Oh, dear! what shall we do!"
But the gingham dog and the calico cat
Wallowed this way and tumbled that,
Employing every tooth and claw
In the awfullest way you ever saw —
And, oh! how the gingham and calico flew!
(Don't fancy I exaggerate —
I got my news from the Chinese plate!)

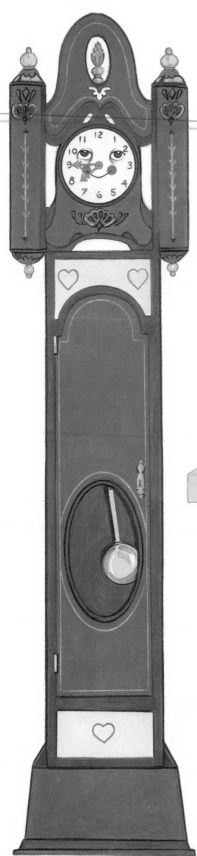

Next morning, where the two had sat
They found no trace of dog or cat,
And some folks think unto this day
That burglars stole that pair away!
But the truth about the cat and pup
Is this: they ate each other up!
Now what do you really think of that!

(The old Dutch clock it told me so,
And that is how I came to know.)

'm Love-a-lot Bear, and I chose this story because it shows that when two people are in love, not even a tall tower nor a mean old witch can keep them from being with each other.

Rapunzel

ONCE THERE WAS a husband and wife who had longed for a child for many years. Finally the happy day arrived when the wife told her husband that they soon would have a baby. They both were terribly happy and looked forward to the baby's arrival.

Then one day the woman was standing at her window, and she saw a beautiful bed of lettuce in the garden of the house next door. It looked so fresh and green that she longed to eat some of it. But she dared not because the garden was owned by an old woman known to be a witch. Her longing increased every day, and since she knew that she would never taste the lettuce, she began to grow pale and weak. Her husband noticed her pale cheeks and became alarmed. "What is the matter, dear wife?" he asked.

"Alas!" she cried. "If I cannot get any of the lettuce from the garden behind the neighboring fence I know that I shall die."

Her husband became greatly alarmed at these words, and he decided that he would fetch her the lettuce. That evening he climbed over the fence into the witch's garden and began to pick the lettuce. He was almost finished when he looked up and was terrified to discover that the witch was standing in front of him.

"Oh, wretched man," cried the witch. "How dare you come into my garden and steal my lettuce? You will be punished for this!"

"Alas," he cried. "Be merciful to me. I came to take the lettuce only because my beloved wife said that she would die unless she could taste it."

Hearing these words, the witch smiled craftily. "If it is as you say, I will allow you to take as much lettuce as you wish, but on one condition. You must give me the child which your wife is about to bring into the world. I will care for it like a mother, and all will be well with it."

The man was so afraid that he consented to the witch's demand. When the baby was born, the witch appeared, gave the child the name of Rapunzel, and took it away with her.

Rapunzel grew to be the most beautiful girl in the country. When she was fourteen years of age, the witch took her and placed her in a high tower that stood in the middle of a dark forest. The tower had neither doors nor stairs and only one small window high up in its wall. Whenever the witch wanted to enter the tower, she would cry, "Rapunzel, Rapunzel, let down your hair!" And Rapunzel, who had beautiful long hair done up in braids, would unfasten it and drop it from the window. Then the witch would climb up Rapunzel's hair and enter the tower.

Although the witch sometimes visited her, Rapunzel was alone for most of her days. She grew lonely and sang to the birds of the forest in the hopes that they would come to visit her. It so happened that one day a prince from a nearby kingdom was riding through the forest when he heard Rapunzel's lovely voice. He rode closer, saw the tower, and was bewitched by her beauty. He wanted to join her but saw that there was no way to enter the tower. He rode home, but he could not forget Rapunzel, so he returned every day to hear her sweet voice and gaze upon her beautiful face.

Then one day he saw the witch approach the tower and cry, "Rapunzel, Rapunzel, let down your hair!" He observed how the witch entered the tower and decided he, too, would climb up the long, long hair.

The prince waited until the old witch had left and then called up to Rapunzel in a voice like that of the witch, "Rapunzel, Rapunzel, let down your hair!" Rapunzel, thinking that the witch had returned, let her hair down from the tower. Quick as a wink, up climbed the prince.

At first Rapunzel was terrified, for she had never seen a man before, but soon her heart was touched by the prince's handsome face and gentle manner. When he asked her to be his bride, she replied, "I will marry you willingly but I do not know how to get down from this tower."

The prince replied, "Whenever I come to visit you I will bring you a piece of silk. If you weave the pieces together, we will soon have a rope that we can climb down." They arranged that the prince would visit Rapunzel at evening, for the witch always came during the day.

The witch discovered nothing of Rapunzel's love for the prince until one day the foolish young maid said, "Old mother, can you tell me why you are so much heavier to draw up into the tower than the young prince who visits me?"

On hearing these words, the witch fell into a rage and cried out, "Oh ungrateful child, you will be punished." She took a pair of scissors and cut off Rapunzel's braids. The next evening when the prince sang out, "Rapunzel, Rapunzel, let down your hair!" the witch shut Rapunzel in a closet and held the braids down in her hands. The prince climbed the tower, but found to his horror that his beloved had been replaced by a snarling old hag. Beside himself with grief, the prince sprang from the tower. He was not killed, but his eyes were scratched out by the thorns into which he fell, and he was blind.

For many months he wandered through the forest until one day he heard the beautiful voice of his beloved Rapunzel. He called out her name, and soon she came running to him, for the witch had been so angry with her that she had put her out into the woods, friendless and alone.

The lovers embraced, but she wept because she saw that he was blind. Two of her tears fell into his eyes, and immediately he could see again.

The lovers rejoiced at the return of his sight, and he took her at once to his kingdom where they were married and lived happily ever after.

'm Wish Bear. This story just makes me feel good. I guess it's because I've always loved to think about kings and knights and princesses. It's so nice to see what happens to the dancing princesses, and the old soldier gets his wish too! Wouldn't you like to walk through a forest where the trees were all golden and then dance all night? I know I would!

The Twelve Dancing Princesses

ONCE UPON A TIME there was a king who had twelve daughters who were so beautiful that he decided to keep their loveliness to himself. He kept them in the castle all day. At night he made them sleep in a long, stone chamber, and he barred and bolted the doors from the outside.

Yet, in spite of this, every morning the princesses' shoes were worn and shabby as if they had been dancing in them all night long. Try as he might, the king could not discover where the princesses went every night and with whom they danced. The king finally became so upset by his daughters' secret that he let it be known that whoever could tell him where his daughters danced every night would be able to choose one of them for his bride.

Many young men of the kingdom traveled to the castle to watch by the princesses' door all night. But each evening before the door was bolted, the oldest of the twelve princesses came out and offered the suitors food and drink that contained a potion, causing them to fall into a deep sleep. So no one discovered the Princesses' secret.

Now in a town not far from the King's castle lived an old soldier. One day while he was walking through the woods he came upon an old woman who was chasing her pig round and round a huge pine tree. Quick as a flash the old soldier pounced on the runaway pig and returned it to the old woman.

"How can I ever thank you?" she said.

"Oh, Granny," he replied, "I want very little in this life, but if I had one thing to wish for, it would be to help the king discover where his daughters dance the night away."

"Well, if that's all you want, it's easy to grant you your wish. Here, take this." She handed him a cloak that she took from her bag. "It's made of fine silk, and when you put it on you will become invisible. Also remember not to eat any tempting sweets and wine that the princesses will offer you. In that way, you will find out where they go each night."

The old soldier thanked the woman and went on his way to the chamber where the princesses were kept each night. The sun set, and before the door was locked the oldest of all the princesses came out and gave the soldier sweet cakes and wine. "Many a man has come to watch us at night, and I know that they often become hungry and thirsty. My sisters think that you look like such a nice man that they would not like that to happen to you."

The soldier thanked her, but he remembered the old woman's advice, so he did not eat or drink. Instead he watched the princesses through a small hole in the wall to their room. At midnight he was amazed to see all twelve of the princesses rise from their beds and put on shimmering, silver gowns. Then the oldest princess clapped her hands. As if by magic, one of the huge pieces of slate in the floor slid aside, and all the princesses descended the narrow staircase that was revealed. The old soldier put on the invisible cloak, quickly unbarred the door of the princesses' room, and followed.

As he crept along, he came too close to the youngest princess and stepped on her gown. She turned in a panic but could see no one behind her. "Oh, help, sisters," she whispered. "I am being clutched by an invisible hand."

But the others only laughed at her and continued on their way. They soon left the staircase and came to a wood where the trees were all made of silver. They passed through it and came to another wood, and there the trees were of gold. They proceeded on and came to a wood where the trees grew precious gems; diamonds on some, emeralds or rubies on the others. And in each wood the old soldier picked a small twig and put it into his pocket. Finally the princesses came to a shoreline and were met by twelve handsome and charming princes, who helped them into boats and rowed for the distant shore. The old soldier, still invisible, got into the last boat with the youngest prince and princess.

"How heavy this boat feels tonight," exclaimed the youngest prince as he rowed, and the youngest princess looked around fearfully to see if anyone else was in the boat. She was sure someone was following her, but she could see nothing.

Finally all the princes and princesses reached a green shore, and there, under a golden moon, they danced and danced until the princesses' slippers were all worn out. When the first rays of dawn streaked the sky the dancing ended, the princesses returned home and went to bed, and all slept soundly until noon.

The old soldier could hardly believe what he had seen, so for the next two nights he again followed the princesses. Sure enough, each night they went to the same spot. It was easy to see that they loved the princes with whom they danced.

After three days, the old soldier went to the king, showed him the twigs from the magical trees, and told him what he had seen. First, however, he made the king promise to forgive his daughters. When the king heard of the hidden staircase and the twelve princes, he fell into a terrible rage, but remembering his promise to the soldier, he calmed himself and said, "Well, old chap, which one of my daughters do you want for a bride?"

The old soldier thought for a moment and then he said, "If it pleases your majesty, I am much too old for any of these fair maidens. Grant my wish and let them marry the handsome princes with whom they dance each night."

"But think of something for yourself, do," insisted the king. The old soldier thought of the old woman who had given him the cloak, and he thought of her pig. "Please, sire, I think I should like a herd of pigs. They are very good and intelligent creatures, and I believe I could be happy tending them for the rest of my days."

And so it came to pass that the twelve dancing princesses married their princes and the old soldier got his pigs, and they all lived happily ever after.

 **I**'m Tenderheart Bear. I've always liked this story because the mysterious helpers seem to have such a good time at what they are doing, and they turn out to be such merry creatures. Doesn't it make you feel good to read about things that turn out well?

The Shoemaker and the Elves

ONCE THERE WAS a shoemaker who fell upon hard times and became so poor that he had nothing left but just enough leather to make one pair of shoes. He cut the leather for the shoes before he went to bed, for he was going to stitch them up and finish them first thing in the morning. Imagine his surprise when he awoke to find the shoes all stitched and ready to be sold! He picked the shoes up and examined them carefully, and sure enough, they were the best shoes ever to come out of his shop.

Just then a customer entered the shop and, seeing the shoes, asked to try them on. He was so pleased by their comfort and good looks that he bought them and gave the shoemaker so much money that the shoemaker could afford to buy leather for four new pairs of shoes.

That night the shoemaker cut the leather for four pairs of shoes and went to sleep. Once again he awoke to find that the leather had been stitched up into the most beautiful shoes that he had ever seen. So it continued. The shoemaker sold the wonderful shoes and got more money for them than he had ever seen in his life. He then bought more leather, which in turn was sewn into shoes during the night. Soon the shoemaker was poor no more. Indeed, he was quite rich.

Still he had no idea who was stitching up the shoes. Then one night right before Christmas his wife said, "Let us sit up tonight and see who is so helpful to us."

The shoemaker agreed. He set out a few candles to light his work room, and then he and his wife hid behind a screen and began to watch. When midnight struck two little men appeared, all dressed in rags. They sat down at the shoemaker's bench and with quick motions stitched up all the leather. They did not stop until all the shoes were finished. When the shoes were all lined up, gleaming in the candle light, the little men jumped up and were gone.

The shoemaker and his wife were amazed by what they had seen, and the wife said, "Now we know whom to thank for our good fortune. Did you see how shabbily they were dressed? Now that winter is here, the poor things must be freezing. In order to thank them for all that they have done for us, I will make them each a new pair of pants, a shirt, and a warm coat."

Her husband agreed that her idea was a good one. Several nights later, instead of putting out the leather, the shoemaker and his wife arranged the clothes all neatly for the elves to find. They then hid behind the screen and waited.

When the little men entered the room that night, they cried out with pleasure as soon as they saw the new clothes. They put them on at once and then began to dance about the room singing, "Clothes like these we've always wished for. Now cobblers we will be no more." Then they laughed and danced out the door.

The shoemaker never saw the elves again, but all went well with his work, and he prospered till the end of his days.

Hush A-Bye

HUSH A-BYE,
Don't you cry,
Go to sleep,
My little baby;
When you wake,
You shall have cake,
And drive those pretty little horses.

Hush a-bye,
Don't you cry,
Go to sleep, my little baby;
Blacks and bays,
Dapples and grays,
And coach and six little horses.

Rock-A-Bye Baby

ROCK-A-BYE BABY, in the tree top,
When the wind blows
The cradle will rock;
When the bough breaks, the cradle will fall,
And down will come baby,
Cradle and all.

Twinkle, Twinkle, Little Star

TWINKLE, TWINKLE, little star,
How I wonder what you are!
Up above the world so high,
Like a diamond in the sky!

When the blazing sun is gone,
When he nothing shines upon,
Then you show your little light,
Twinkle, twinkle, all the night.

Hush Little Baby

H USH, LITTLE BABY, don't say a word,
Mama's going to buy you a mockingbird.

And if that mockingbird don't sing,
Mama's going to buy you a diamond ring.

And if that diamond ring turns brass,
Mama's going to buy you a looking glass.

And if that looking glass gets broke,
Mama's going to buy you a billy goat.

And if that billy goat won't pull,
Mama's going to buy you a cart and bull.

If that cart and bull turn over,
Mama's going to buy you a dog named Rover.

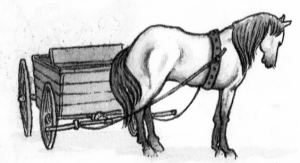

If that dog named Rover won't bark,
Mama's going to buy you a horse and cart.

If that horse and cart fall down,
You'll still be the prettiest girl in town.

ince I was the one who thought of collecting these stories, I get to pick the last one. "Sleeping Beauty" has always been one of my favorite stories. When I shut my eyes, I can almost see the beautiful princess, and best of all it's about something I know lots about — sleeping!

The Sleeping Beauty

ONCE THERE WAS a king and queen who were very sad because they had no children. At last, however, the queen did have a baby — a little girl. To celebrate his daughter's birth the king gave a splendid christening party, and he made all the fairies of the kingdom godmothers to the princess so that each of them could give her a wonderful gift.

On the day of the christening there was a great banquet in honor of the fairies. But just as everyone sat down, in came an old fairy whom the king had completely forgotton to invite. The king quickly laid a place for her, but the old fairy felt that she had been insulted and began to grumble to herself in a most threatening way. The youngest of all the fairies heard her and, fearing that the old fairy might give the princess an unlucky gift, hid behind the curtains in order to ensure that the old fairy would not be the last to present her gift.

The fairies then began to give the princess their presents. One said that the princess would be the most beautiful girl in the world, the next that she would sing as sweetly as a bird, another that she would be graceful. And so it went, each fairy presenting a marvelous gift.

Then it was the old fairy's turn. Eyes flashing in anger, she said that the princess would prick herself on a spinning wheel, and that injury would be the death of her. They all cried out when they heard of this terrible gift, but at that moment the youngest fairy stepped from behind the curtains and said in a loud voice, "Do not be afraid, for here is my gift. The princess will not die but instead will only fall into a deep sleep that will last one hundred years. At the end of that time a prince will come and wake her."

Despite the young fairy's words, the king was terrified of the curse and had all the spinning wheels in the kingdom burned in a huge bonfire. He watched his daughter carefully, but one day, after fifteen years had passed, he and the queen went to visit one of their country houses and left the princess alone for the day.

The princess roamed about the palace and finally wandered up into one of the towers. There she found a little attic. In it an old woman sat spinning.

"What are you doing?" asked the princess.

"Why, spinning, my pretty thing," answered the old woman.

At that moment the king and queen returned and began calling for their daughter. The princess paid no attention to her parents' call but reached out and said, "How do you do it? Here, let me spin."

No sooner had she taken hold of the spinning wheel than she pricked her finger and fell down in a deep sleep. When the princess closed her eyes, her enchantment bewitched all the others in the castle, and they too closed their eyes and slept.

One hundred years went by, and a great forest of thorns and brambles grew up around the castle. Then one day a prince from a neighboring country saw the castle's towers as he was out hunting. He asked who lived in the castle. Everyone who answered told him that it was a haunted castle in which an ogre lived. Finally one old man said, "Your highness, I have heard it said that there is a princess in that castle who sleeps until some brave prince comes to her rescue."

Hearing this, the prince at once decided to try and see the princess. No sooner did he approach the forest than all the thorns and brambles parted to let him pass. He came to the courtyard, and the sight that met his view was a terrible one. Everywhere he looked men and women were sprawled as if dead. When he looked more closely, however, their pink cheeks told him that they were just asleep.

He left the courtyard and climbed up the tower stairs. He came to the attic room, and there he saw the most beautiful sight of his whole life. The princess, dressed in a velvet gown, lay on a small cot. The light from the window made her hair seem like spun gold. The prince bent to admire her and, overwhelmed by her beauty, kissed her gently. The princess awoke and seeing him said, "Is it you, my prince? I have dreamed about you."

The prince and princess went down to the courtyard, where the others were also waking up. The king ordered a great feast, and within the week he had granted his consent to the marriage of the prince and princess. They were married on a beautiful spring day and they lived happily ever after.

Wynken, Blynken and Nod

by Eugene Field

WYNKEN, BLYNKEN AND NOD one night
   Sailed off in a wooden shoe —
Sailed on a river of crystal light
   Into a sea of dew.
"Where are you going, and what do you wish?"
   The old moon asked the three.
"We have come to fish for the herring fish
   That live in this beautiful sea;
Nets of silver and gold have we!"
      Said Wynken,
      Blynken,
      And Nod.

The old moon laughed and sang a song
As they rocked in a wooden shoe,
And the wind that sped them all night long
Ruffled the waves of dew.
The little stars were the herring fish
That lived in that beautiful sea—
"Now cast your nets wherever you wish,
Never afeared are we;"
So cried the stars to the fishermen three,
Wynken,
Blynken,
and Nod.

All night long their nets they threw
To the stars in the twinkling foam—
Then down from the skies came the wooden shoe,
Bringing the fishermen home;
'Twas all so pretty a sail it seemed
As if it could not be,
And some folks thought 'twas a dream they'd dreamed
Of sailing that beautiful sea—
But I shall name you the fishermen three:
Wynken,
Blynken,
and Nod.

Wynken and Blynken are two little eyes,
And Nod is a little head,
And the wooden ship that sailed the skies
Is a wee one's trundle bed.
So shut your eyes while mother sings
Of wonderful sights that be
And you shall see the beautiful things
As you rock in the misty sea,
Where the old shoe rocked the fishermen three:
Wynken,
Blynken,
And Nod.

Good night, sleep tight. We love you.

(signed) Care Bears